The Golden Goose

Based on a story by the Brothers Grimm

Retold by Conrad Mason

Illustrated by
Mike and Carl Gordon

Reading Consultant: Alison Kelly
Roehampton University

This story is about
a woodcutter,

his three
sons,

a little
old man,

a golden goose,

an innkeeper and his wife,

their three daughters

and a very
sad princess.

There was once
a woodcutter,

who had three sons.

Ronald was strong.

Donald was handsome.

But Billy...

...wasn't strong
OR handsome.

One day, the woodcutter
became ill.

"Who will go to
the forest to chop
wood?" he said.

"I will," said Ronald.

After all, I am the oldest.

So off he went.

He chopped

and chopped.

And then
he sat down
for lunch.

As he ate, a little old man popped up beside him.

"Please can you spare some food?" he asked.

"Get your own food!"
snapped Ronald.

12

"Suit yourself," said the little old man.

And he vanished.

13

The next morning,
Ronald had a shock.
He itched all over.

He itched...

and scratched...

...and ITCHED!

14

"I can't go to the forest like this," he howled.

15

So Donald went instead.
After chopping...

and chopping...

he sat down for lunch.

All of a sudden, the little old man appeared. "May I have a bite?" he asked.

"No way," snorted Donald.

The little old man
shook his head
and vanished.

The next morning,
Donald had a shock...

"I can't go to the forest like this," he wailed.

You'll have to go, Billy.

So Billy went instead.

At lunchtime,
Billy sat down
to eat.

The little old man
popped up again.

"Please will you share your food with me?" he begged.

"Thank you," said the little old man.

"Now, chop down this tree and see what happens."

And with that,
he was gone.

25

Billy chopped down
the tree.

CREAK!

There, in the trunk sat...

...a *golden goose!*

Billy picked it up and set
off for home.

But he got lost.

Night came,
and he stopped
at an inn.

"What a fine goose!"
said the innkeeper.

"Thank you,"
said Billy, and
he went to bed.

29

Much later, the innkeeper's eldest daughter crept into Billy's room.

She wanted a golden feather.

But as soon as she
touched the goose...

...she stuck to it!

Her two sisters ran in.

They tried to help...

...but they stuck too.

Billy woke up and got
a shock.

He tugged the goose,
and he stuck as well.

"Oh well," he said. "We'll just have to stay together." And he went back to bed.

The next morning,
Billy set off with
his goose...

...and the
three girls.

"Girls! Where are you going?" shouted the innkeeper's wife.

She grabbed at her youngest daughter...

...and she stuck fast.

"I'll help!" called the innkeeper. He grabbed his wife...

...but he stuck too.

"Oh dear," said Billy.
"You'll have to come with
me as well."

Soon they came
to a castle.

A princess lived in this
castle, and she never,
ever smiled.

But when she saw
the innkeeper...

his wife...

and the
three sisters...

all running behind
Billy and his goose...

...she started
to smile.

Then she burst
out laughing.

"At last!" cried the king.
"Young man, would you
like to marry
my daughter?"

You can marry
her today!

"Yes please!" said Billy.

The little old man
appeared at the
wedding.

He waved his hands...

...and everyone
came un-stuck.

The Golden Goose was first written down by two brothers, Jacob and Wilhelm Grimm, about two hundred years ago. The Grimm brothers lived in Germany and collected lots of folk tales.

Designed by Louise Flutter
Series designer: Russell Punter
Series editor: Lesley Sims

First published in 2008 by Usborne Publishing Ltd., Usborne House, 83-85 Saffron Hill, London EC1N 8RT, England. www.usborne.com
Copyright © 2008 Usborne Publishing Ltd.